Spots
OR
STRIPES?

VASANTI UNKA

t

templar publishing

Deep in the jungle,
all was at peace.

Until Tiger and Leopard
started to squabble.

Stripes are more
handsome than spots,
don't you think?

The squabble turned into a quarrel.

But stripes are so **BOLD**. Spots have stripes RULE STRIPES!

PIZZAZZ.

THE WORLD!

SPOTS ARE THE TOPS!

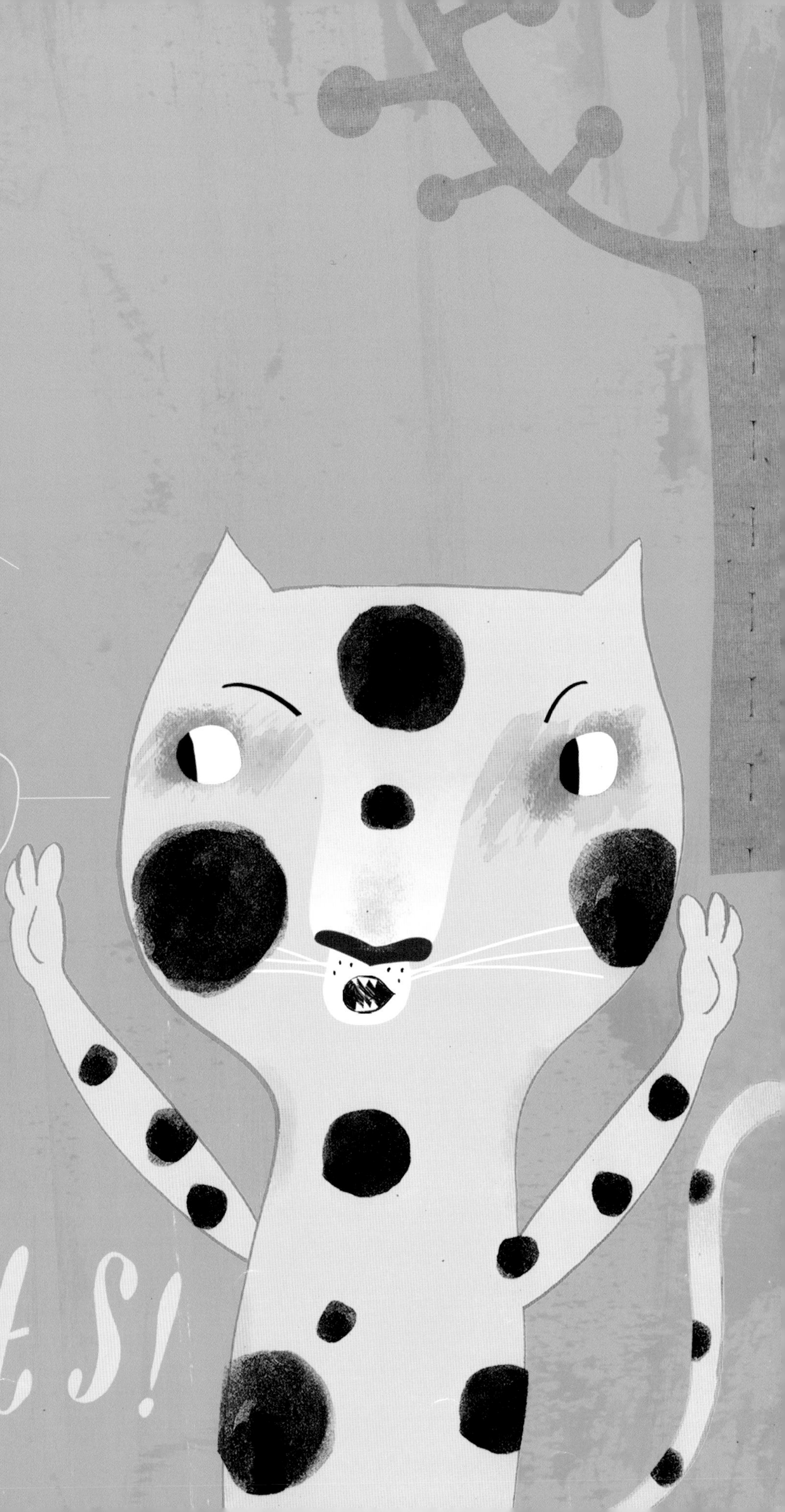

NO, SPOTS!

The quarrel turned into a fight.

STRIPES!

Banana-skin missiles
and mucky mud bombs
flew through the air.

And the fight became a …

Rotten tomatoes
and smelly old eggs
exploded on trees.

By lunchtime,
the jungle was a mess.

So Monkey yelled,

CEASE

And the Jungle Council called a meeting.

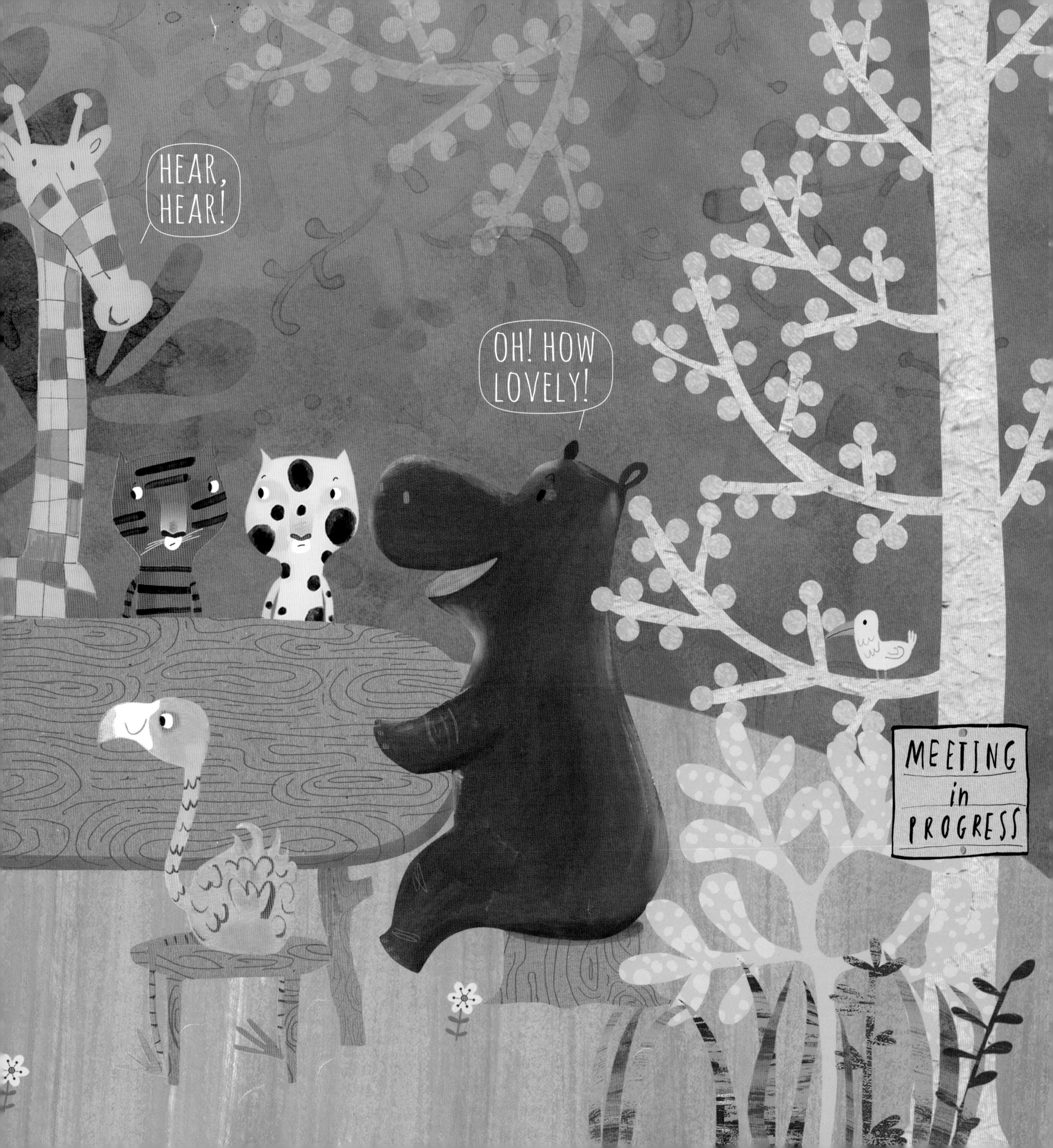
HEAR, HEAR!
OH! HOW LOVELY!
MEETING in PROGRESS

the JUN

A HUGE ROUND OF APPLAUSE FOR ALL THE CONTESTANTS!

the JUDGES

The following day ...

PEACEFUL
JUNGLE
CONTEST
—————
ALL WELCOME
—————
WHEN: NOW
WHERE: HERE

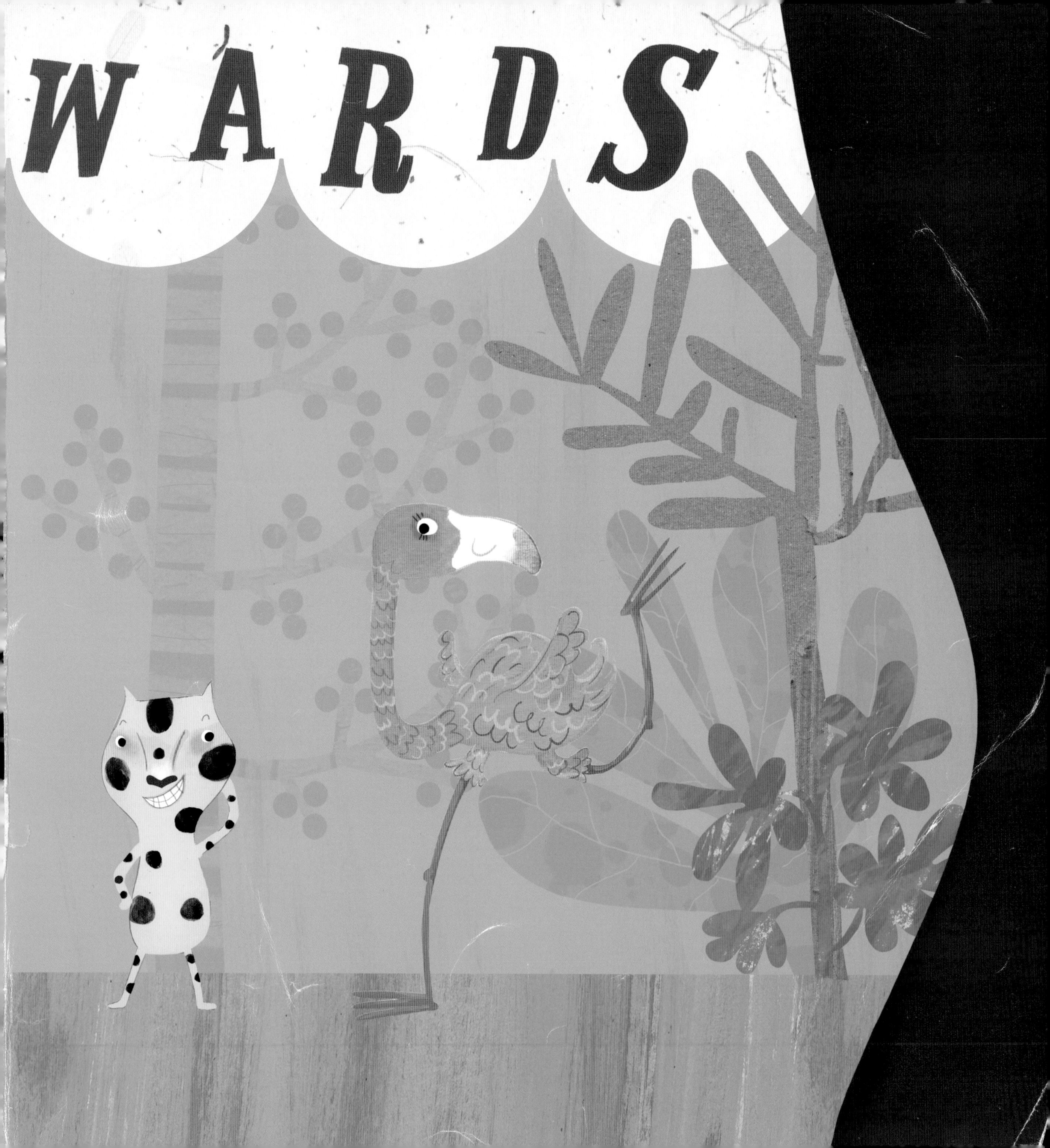
WARDS

Then the judges announced their favourites …

They liked Elephant's elegant suit.

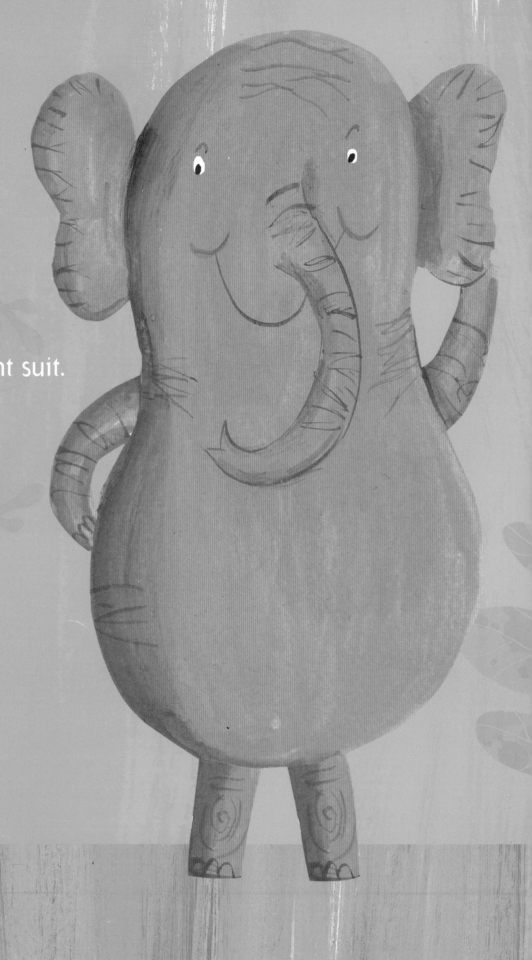

WRINKLES ARE ALL THE RAGE!

And the nature expert's green jacket.

WILD!

They were impressed with Tortoise's hardy shell.

A Bulletproof BACKPACK!

And admired Giraffe's chequered coat.

CHEEKY CHECKS!

Hippopotamus was praised for her swanky swimsuit.

DRIP-DRY TOGS ARE VERY HIP!

And Peacock for his
multicoloured attire.

They loved Tiger's splendid stripes
and Leopard's fabulous spots.

Spots and stripes
are always stylish!

Especially when
they're together.

But they ADORED
Flamingo's fluffy,
pink plumage.

Deep in the jungle,
all was at peace.

Well, sort of …

DJ HIP STAR